# Johnny Optimism

## LAUGHTER IS DEBASED MEDICINE

# Volume Two

CREATED WITH COMIC LIFE BY PLASQ.COM

ISBN: 9798648449947

SKLITCH
SKLITCH
SKLITCH

# Opening Remarks

WELCOME TO THE SECOND OMNIBUS COLLECTION OF *JOHNNY OPTIMISM* CARTOONS! ANOTHER 600 (COUNT 'EM!) VISITS TO AN UNNAMED, OFF-KILTER HOSPITAL FILLED WITH STRANGE DIAGNOSES, UNLIKELY AILMENTS, PSYCHOLOGICAL DISORDERS, DIMWITTED DOCTORS, MONKEYS, CLOWNS, AND UNENDING WAVES OF HILARIOUSLY BAD NEWS. AT THE CENTER OF WHICH IS AN ALWAYS-OPTIMISTIC BOY AND HIS FAITHFUL DOG.

AFTER TEN YEARS, I DON'T REALLY FEEL LIKE I WRITE THESE CARTOONS ANYMORE. RATHER, I JUST DROP IN TO JOHNNY'S WORLD AND SURROUND MYSELF WITH THE CHARACTERS, THEN WAIT FOR THEM TO TALK TO ME AND SAY SOMETHING FUNNY. OR HORRIBLE. OR USUALLY BOTH. SO IF YOU HATE A PARTICULAR CARTOON OR FIND IT BEYOND THE PALE, DON'T BLAME ME... BLAME MY MISCHIEVOUS TWO-DIMENSIONAL CO-WRITERS.

AS I WRITE THIS INTRODUCTION, WE FIND OURSELVES IN THE MIDST (OR IS IT STILL JUST THE BEGINNING?) OF THE CORONAVIRUS CRISIS OF 2020. THERE IS FEAR, CONFUSION, A HOST OF UNSOLVED MEDICAL MYSTERIES, AND AN ANXIETY-PRODUCING UNCERTAINTY ABOUT THE FUTURE. IT MAY SEEM LIKE WE'RE ALL LIVING IN JOHNNY'S WORLD NOW...BUT THE TRUTH IS THAT HE'S BEEN LIVING IN *OUR* WORLD ALL ALONG.

IT'S A WORLD THAT ISN'T REALLY SAFE, PERFECT, OR PREDICTABLE. BUT IT'S ALSO A WORLD OF LOVE, FRIENDSHIPS, AND LAUGHTER. AND THAT LAUGHTER IS A POWERFUL THING...ESPECIALLY WHEN WE CHOOSE TO LAUGH IN THE FACE OF THAT WHICH WOULD DEFEAT US. IT GIVES US THE STRENGTH TO CARRY ON AND ENJOY THE MANY GOOD ASPECTS OF LIFE THAT ARE ALWAYS PRESENT WHATEVER OUR CIRCUMSTANCES.

QUITE SIMPLY, LAUGHTER HELPS US COPE. AND AS JOHNNY SAYS, "COPE SPRINGS ETERNAL."

SO ENJOY THESE CARTOONS, SECURE IN THE KNOWLEDGE THAT THEY'RE NOT ABOUT MOCKING ANYONE'S MISFORTUNES OR MALADIES, AND THAT NEITHER YOU NOR I ARE TERRIBLE PEOPLE FOR LAUGHING.

WE JUST NEED TO REMEMBER TO *KEEP* LAUGHING WHEN THE JOKE IS ON US.

Stilton Jarlsberg

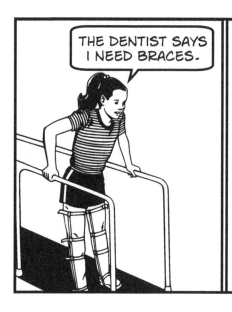

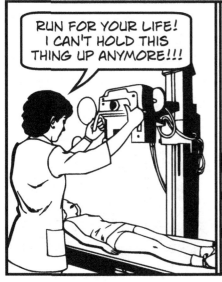

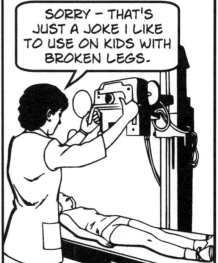

THE DOCUMENTARY MAKER...

SO JOHNNY, JUST HOW DO YOU KEEP YOUR SPIRITS UP?

WELL, MY DOCTORS HELP ME KEEP THINGS IN PERSPECTIVE...

WHENEVER I FEEL BAD, THEY SAY I SHOULD CONSIDER YOUTH IN ASIA.

I THINK OUR NEW HOSPITAL COOK HAS A BAD SKIN CONDITION.

WHAT MAKES YOU SAY THAT?

TODAY'S BREAKFAST WAS BACON AND ECZEMA.

I TOOK YOUR ADVICE, BUT HE JUST WON'T EAT STRANGE VEGETABLES.

I SAID "STRAINED" VEGETABLES.

HEAR THAT, SWEETIE? NO MORE RUTABAGAS FROM CHERNOBYL!

THE DOCUMENTARY MAKER...

AND HERE'S THE JOLLY CLOWN WHO KEEPS THE SICK KIDS LAUGHING!

SAY – HAVEN'T I SEEN THOSE GIRLS BEFORE?

MAYBE.

HAVE YOU BOUGHT MILK RECENTLY?

YOU'RE WELL ON YOUR WAY TO GROWING UP TO BE A PIRATE!

WHY WOULD I WANT TO BE A PIRATE?

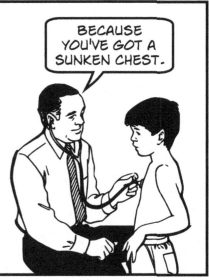

BECAUSE YOU'VE GOT A SUNKEN CHEST.

HEY, HERE COMES A NEW KID!

WHAT ARE YOU IN FOR?

I'M A RINGWORM BEARER.

DUDE – STYLE POINTS!

THANKS.

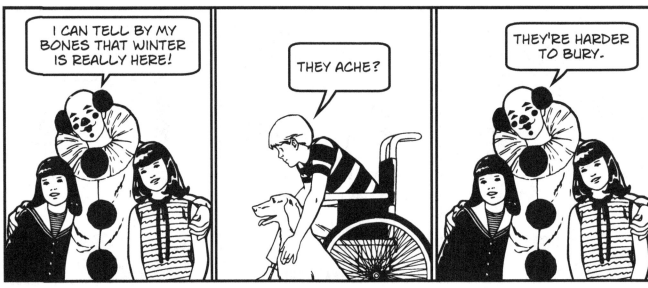

NOTE: PHARMY THE DINOSAUR IS IN NO WAY RELATED TO BARNEY™ THE LOVABLE NON-LITIGIOUS TV DINOSAUR

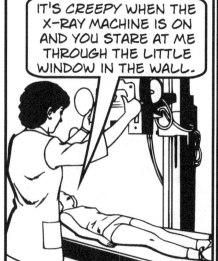

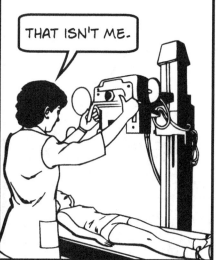

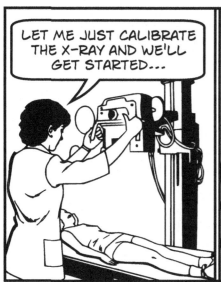

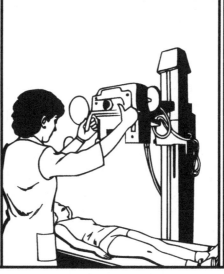

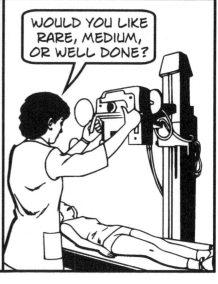

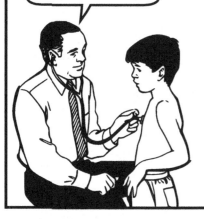

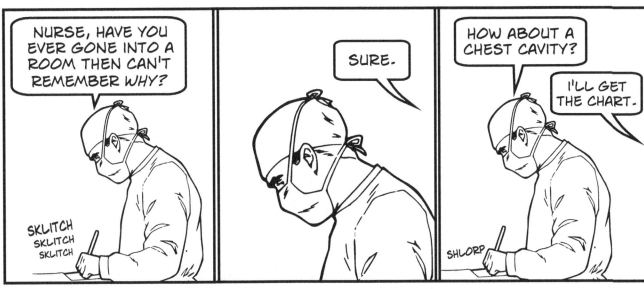

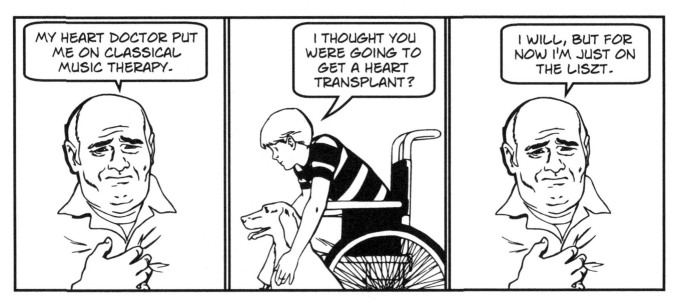

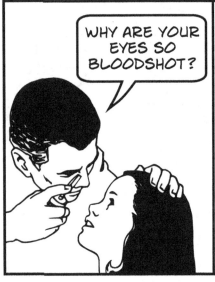

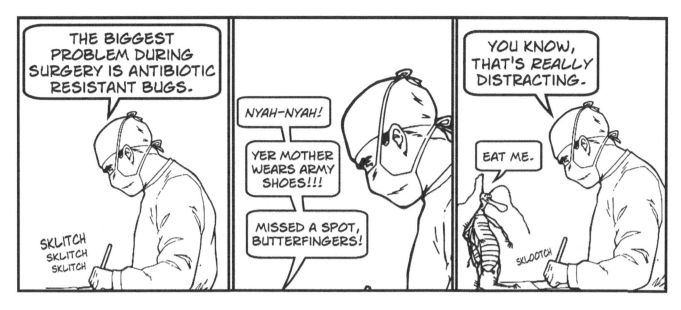

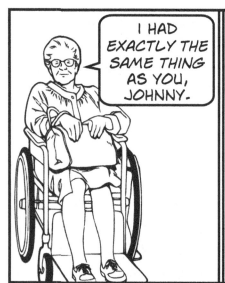

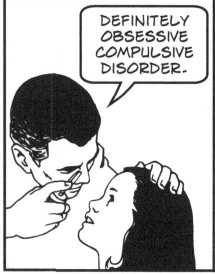

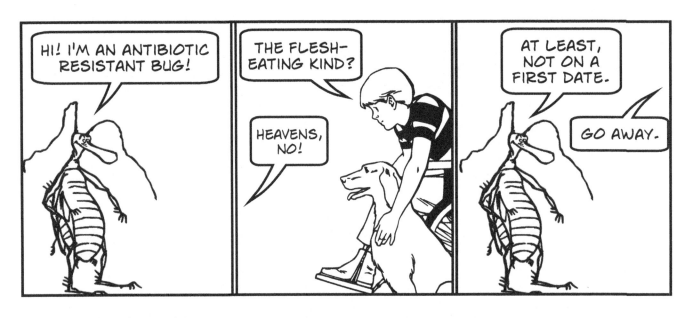

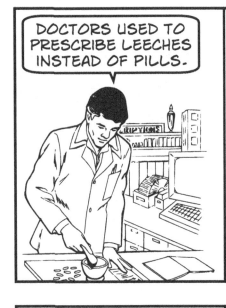

THE PATHOLOGICAL LIAR

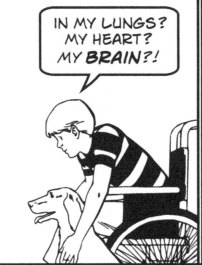

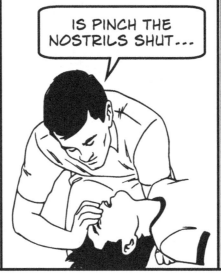

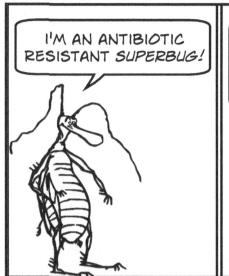

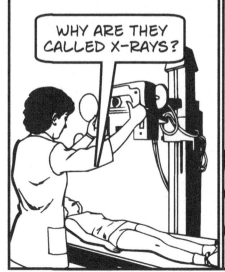

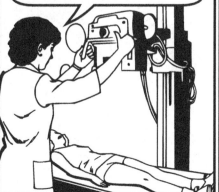

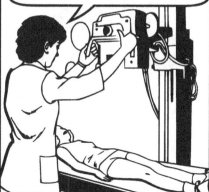

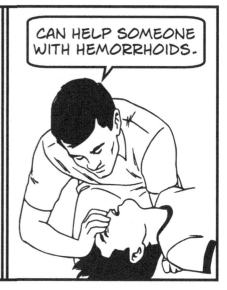

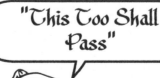

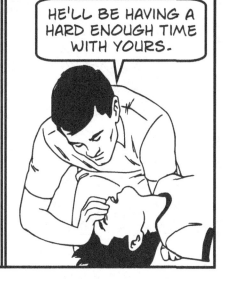

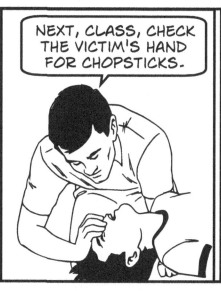

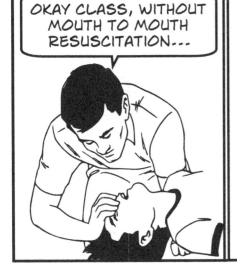

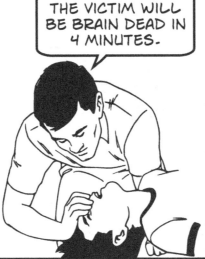

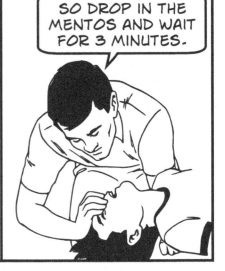

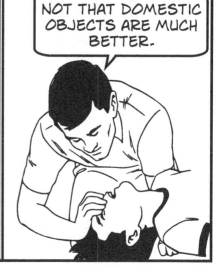

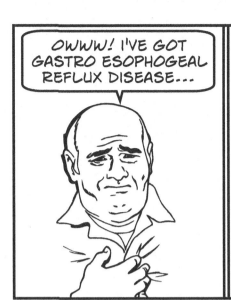

SO, LITTLE MISSY, YOU SAY YOU'RE INTERESTED IN DUCK HUNTIN'?

NO, I SAID MR. DUCK IS INTERESTED IN HUNTING.

BITTY BUGS OR WIGGLE WORMS?

MOUNTAIN LIONS OR ESCAPED CONVICTS.

I DON'T MUCH COTTON TO HOW HE'S LOOKIN' AT ME...

PEPE THE EPILEPTIC

I HEARD YOU HAD A BIG SEIZURE AT THE CORRAL.

NO, BUT THAT'S WHAT EVERYONE THOUGHT FOR 15 MINUTES...

TILL THE ELECTRIC FENCE I'D GRABBED FINALLY SHORTED OUT.

OUCH.

HELP! A RATTLESNAKE BIT MY PRIVATES WHEN I WAS TAKING A LEAK!

YOU'VE GOT TO SUCK OUT THE POISON!

WE DON'T HAVE ANY RATTLESNAKES.

WELL, IT MIGHT HAVE BEEN A STAPLER...

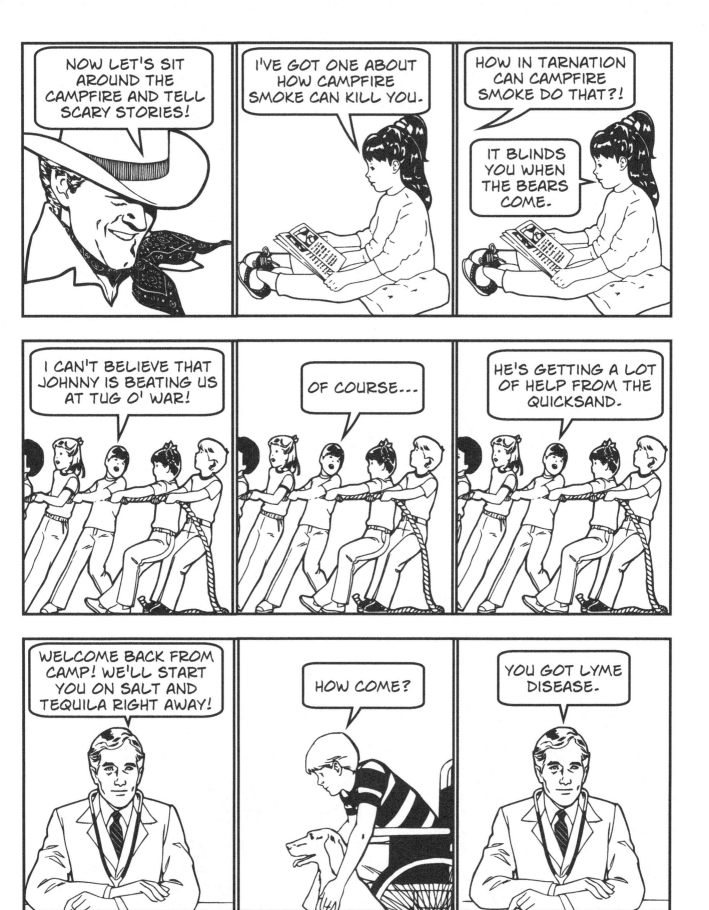

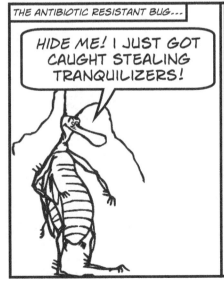

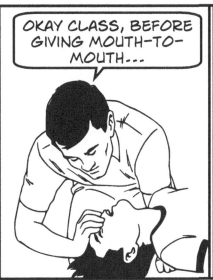

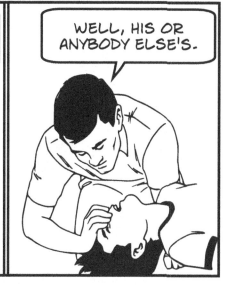

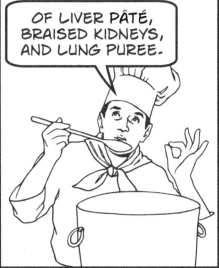

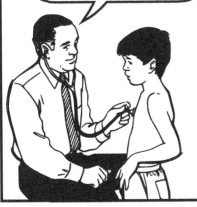

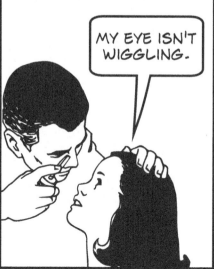

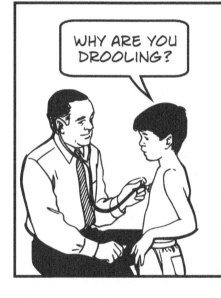

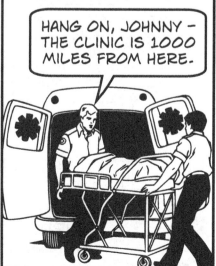

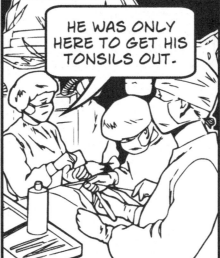

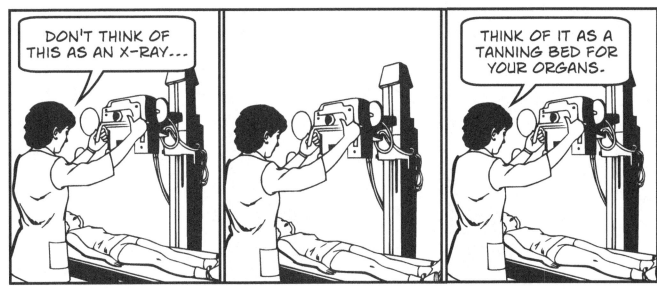

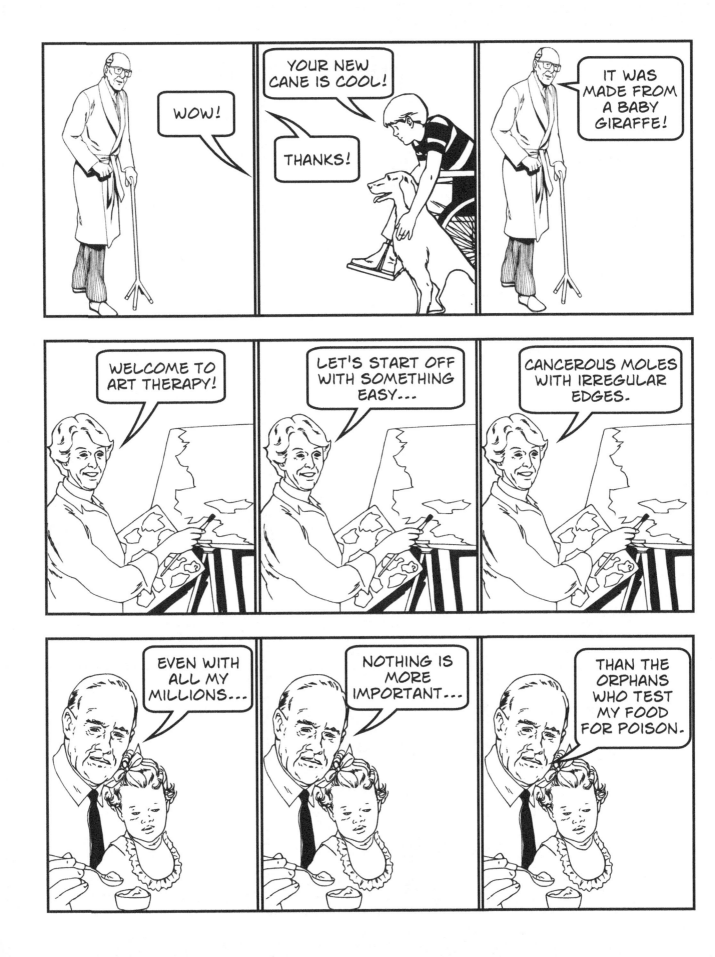

I HAD TERRIBLE SNIFFLING AND SNEEZING AND COUGHING AND A SORE THROAT...

MY EYES BURNED AND I HAD A POUNDING SINUS HEADACHE...

AND MY FEVER HIT 104!

NAVAJO COLD TALKER.

TOE TAG!

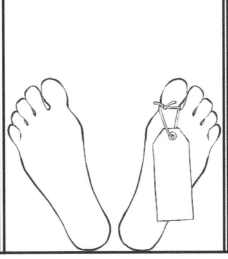

YOU'RE "IT!"

I WONDER IF THIS IS HOW GOD FEELS WHEN HE MAKES PEOPLE?

ALL POWERFUL?

NO...

LIKE HE NEEDS TO SCRATCH HIS NOSE BUT DOESN'T WANT GOO ON HIM.

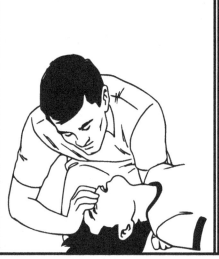

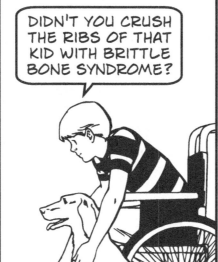

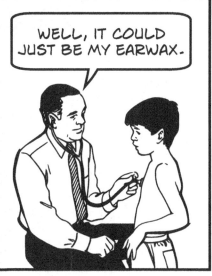

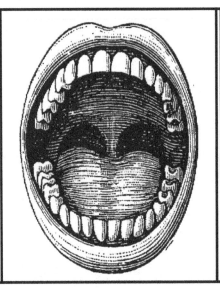

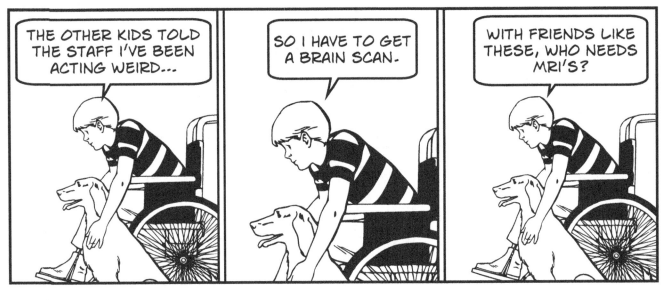

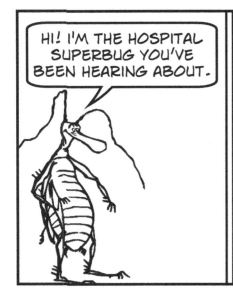

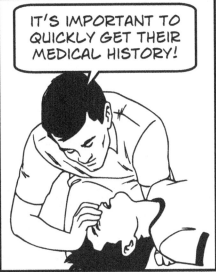

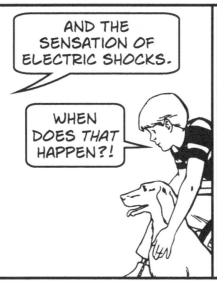

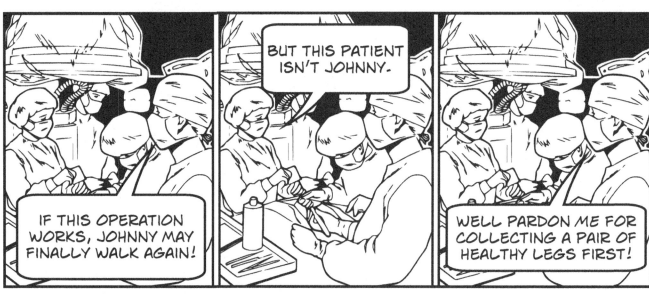

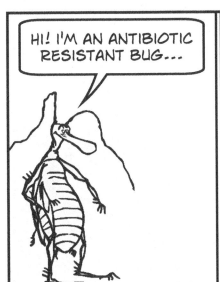

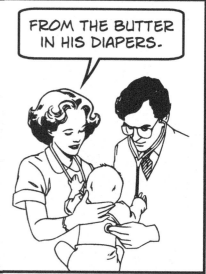

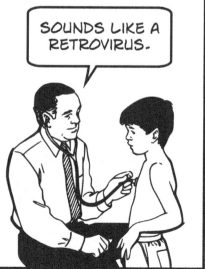

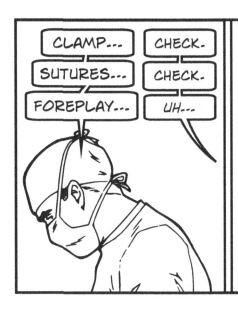

THE CARDIOLOGIST SAYS I'M GETTING A NEW LEASE ON LIFE.

SO YOU'RE BETTER?

NO – HE'S PUTTING ME ON A RENTED HEART-LUNG MACHINE.

TIME FOR YOUR SHOT – MAKE A FIST!

WHY?

BECAUSE IT'S NOT FAIR TO STAB SOMEONE WHO CAN'T FIGHT BACK.

A MAN THOUGHT HE WAS A CLOCK. ALL HE EVER SAID WAS TICK TICK TICK.

BUT THE DOCTORS HELPED HIM?

OH, YES...

THEY HAD WAYS OF MAKING HIM TOCK.

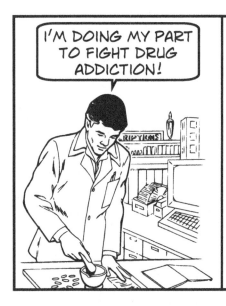

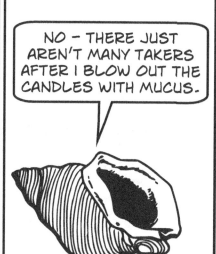

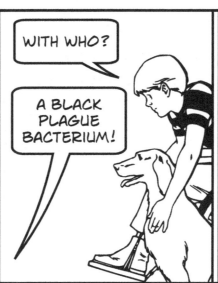

THE DOCTOR SAID I NEEDED AN EMOTIONAL SUPPORT ANIMAL.

WHAT HE LACKS IN WARMTH, HE MAKES UP IN ATTENTIVENESS.

JOHNNY, YOU MAY BE DYING, BUT HOPE SPRINGS ETERNAL.

"HOPE SPRINGS ETERNAL?"

THAT'S THE GOLF TOURNAMENT I'M ATTENDING NEXT WEEK.

THE LAB RAT...

SCIENTISTS HIT MY FOOT WITH A HAMMER TO SEE IF IT WORKS AS BIRTH CONTROL.

AND DOES IT?

WELL, IT DID MAKE ME LIMP.

I'LL BET!

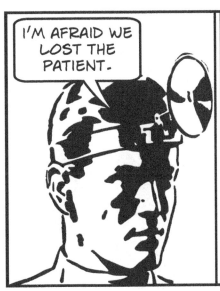

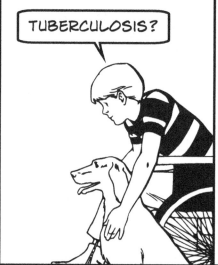

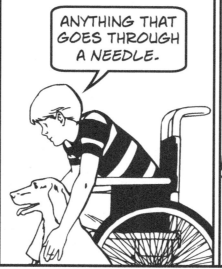

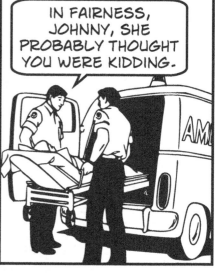

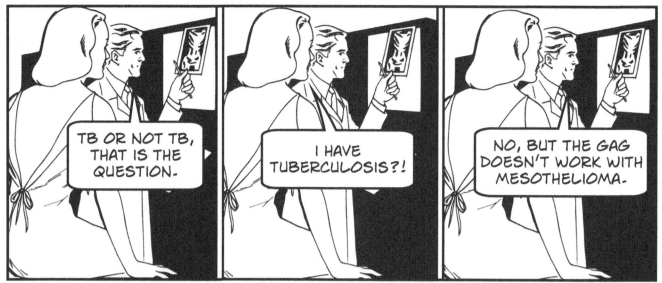

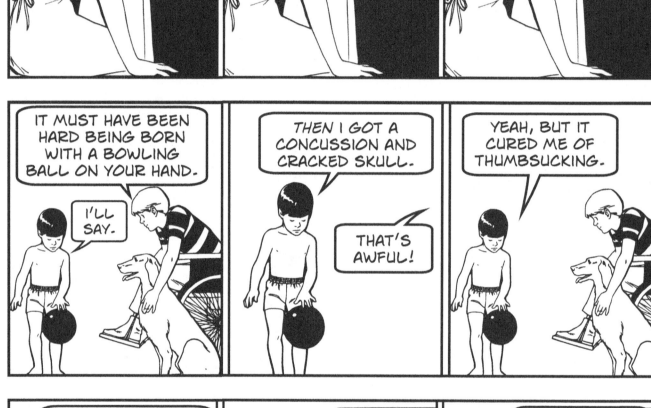

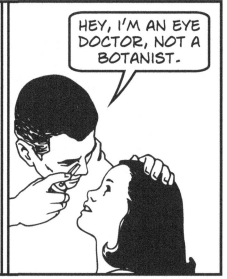

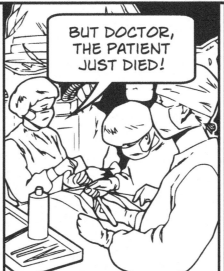

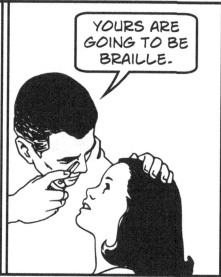

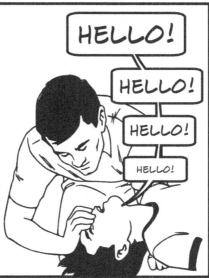

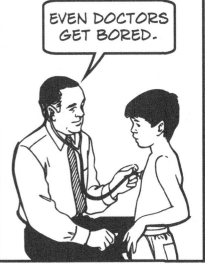

Made in the USA
Middletown, DE
20 September 2020